P9-AQA-058

When Mommy Is Sick

Ferne Sherkin-Langer

illustrations by Kay Life

Albert Whitman & Company, Morton Grove, Illinois

The text typeface is Bembo.
The illustration medium is watercolor.
The design is by Karen A. Yops.

Library of Congress Cataloging-in-Publication Data
Sherkin-Langer, Ferne.
When Mommy is sick / written by Ferne Sherkin-Langer;
illustrated by Kay Life.
p.   cm.
Summary: When Mommy is in the hospital, as she is
frequently sick, her child misses her a lot.
ISBN 0-8075-8894-6
[1. Mother and child—Fiction. 2. Sick—Fiction.]
I. Life, Kay, ill. II. Title.
PZ7.S54516Wh   1995   94-26163
[E]—dc20   CIP
                                                      AC

To Jessica, Benjamin, and Alexander,
who are my inspiration.

F.S-L.

With appreciation and gratitude
to Noble Hospital, Westfield, Massachusetts,
and York Hospital, York, Maine.

K.L.

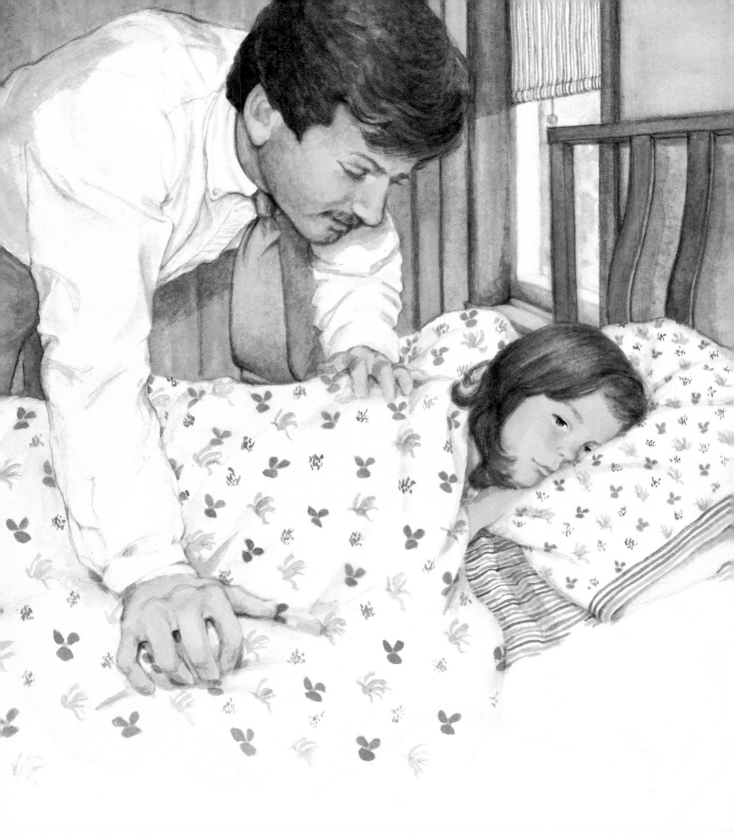

Sometimes when my mommy gets sick she has
to go and live in the hospital.

Today Daddy comes to get me out of bed. And I
remember that Mommy isn't here because she's sick again.
It makes me feel sad.

Charlotte, my babysitter, makes my breakfast. She
always puts on the strawberry jam too thick and cuts my
toast in triangles. Mommy knows how much jam I like
and how to cut my toast in squares. But Mommy isn't
here.

Charlotte drives me to school. When I'm there
I don't feel like singing at music time. I don't feel like
making pictures or playing with my friends. My teacher
asks me if I would like to make a picture for my mommy.
I draw a picture of Mommy and me holding hands. I use
lots of red because red is Mommy's favorite color.

After school Daniel's mommy takes me to the playground and pushes me on my favorite swing. I really like Daniel's mommy. But it isn't fair! She's almost never sick. Why does *my* mommy always have to get sick?

It feels like Mommy has been in the hospital for three whole years, but Daddy tells me it has only been three days. I'm scared that she'll never come home.

When Daddy comes home from work, he tells me that I can visit Mommy with him on Saturday.

I ask Daddy, "How many more days till Saturday?"

Daddy and I make a calendar. He shows me where Saturday is and how to cross off the days of the week.

Sometimes I think that Mommy has to go to the hospital because I did something bad. Last week when she made me go to my room, I wished that she would just go away.

So I ask Daddy, "If you wish something bad about somebody, can it come true?"

"Our wishes come from how we feel about things," he says. "Wishes can't make something happen. It's nobody's fault that Mommy is sick."

Every night before I go to bed, I call Mommy to say goodnight. Daddy and I cross off one more day. Saturday is almost here.

On Saturday morning Daddy and I drive to the hospital. I remember to bring Mommy the picture I made in school.

We wait for the elevator to take us to Mommy's room. She's always on the seventh floor. I can hardly wait to see her! When we get into the elevator the number seven light is already on.

"That's okay," Daddy says, "you can push it anyway."

I hold Daddy's hand and pull him down the hallway to Mommy's room. A nurse I have seen before smiles at me. I smile back.

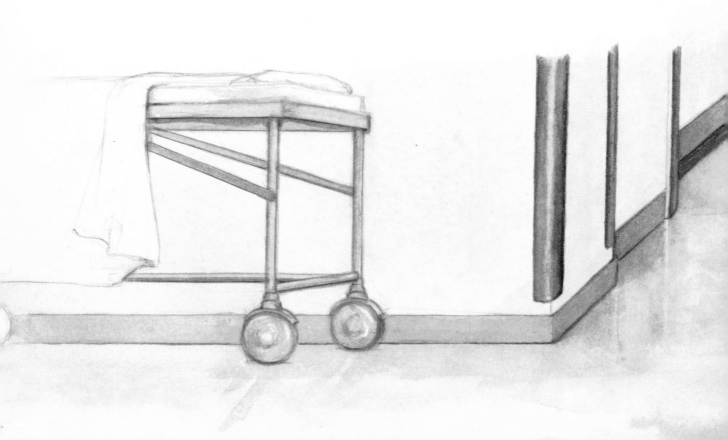

"Here we are," Daddy says. Mommy is lying down. I give her the picture I made for her. It makes Mommy smile, and I feel good. Then Daddy hangs the picture on the wall where everybody can see it.

"Come here and give me a hug, sweetie," Mommy says.

Sometimes I'm afraid to hug Mommy. Will my hug hurt her? I look at her very closely. Her face looks like her regular face, so I give her a big squeezer.

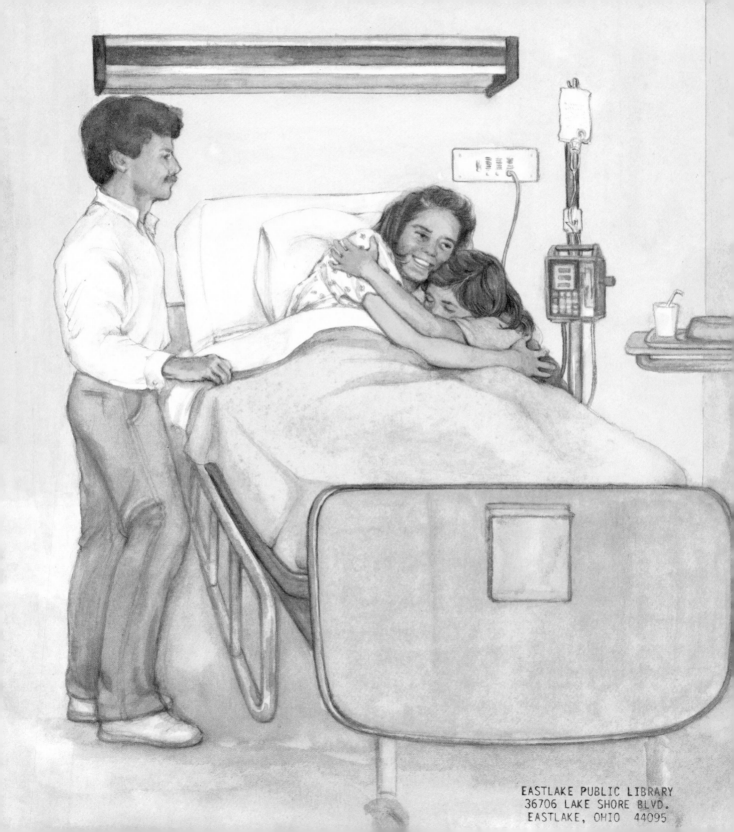

Every time Mommy has to be in the hospital, her room looks the same. She has a special drawer where I keep some of my favorite toys—my green racing car, my doll with blue eyes that open and shut, and my striped bag filled to the top with crayons and markers. I like to play with my toys in Mommy's room in my very own spot.

But sometimes I don't feel like playing. Mommy's bed is big and far from the floor, but if she is not feeling too sick, I climb up and sit on her lap and she reads me a story. I pretend we are at home again. I like to pretend that.

Soon Daddy says it is time to go home. I give Mommy a hug and kiss and wave goodbye. I try not to cry. I hate saying goodbye to Mommy.

On the way home I tell Daddy that when I grow up I am going to be a doctor so I can make Mommy better.

On Monday Charlotte comes to take care of me again.
She brings puzzles for us to do together, but it doesn't
make me miss Mommy any less. I pretend that every
piece I fit together makes Mommy a little bit better.

The next night Daddy comes home from work and tells me that Mommy is coming home this Saturday. Each night after my telephone kiss from Mommy, I cross the day off the calendar: Tuesday, Wednesday, Thursday, Friday . . .

Saturday morning Daddy and I get ready together. "Today is the day Mommy's coming home!" I shout. I want everybody in the whole world to know. Daddy helps me make a big welcome home sign, and we put it on the front door so Mommy can see it as soon as she gets home.

Mommy is home! But Daddy says that she still needs
to rest. She rests for Sunday, Monday, Tuesday, Wednesday,
Thursday, Friday . . .

But on Saturday, Mommy takes me to the playground.
She pushes me on my favorite swing and catches me at the
bottom of the slide.

When we get home she makes me a sandwich for
lunch. She puts just the right amount of jam on it, and
cuts it up into squares.

At bedtime Mommy reads me a story, then she gives
me a hug and kiss. She pulls the blankets up to my chin.
"Have a good sleep," Mommy says.
"Will you be here when I wake up?" I ask.
"I sure will," she says.
I close my eyes and feel happy all over.